Rose Gold
and friends

Published in the UK by Scholastic Children's Books, 2020
Euston House, 24 Eversholt Street, London, NW1 1DB, UK
A division of Scholastic Limited.

London – New York – Toronto – Sydney – Auckland
Mexico City – New Delhi – Hong Kong

SCHOLASTIC and associated logos are trademarks and/or
registered trademarks of Scholastic Inc.

ISBN 978 1407 19671 8

A CIP catalogue record for this book is available from the British Library.

Printed by CPI Group (UK) Ltd, Croydon, CR0 4YY
Papers used by Scholastic Children's Books are made
from wood grown in sustainable forests.

1 3 5 7 9 10 8 6 4 2

www.scholastic.co.uk

for Peggy (and family)

Rose Gold
and friends

Oralies Scavenger Hunt

ALICE HEMMING

■SCHOLASTIC

Chapter 1

A Barking Beige Bundle

Amber, Yasmeen and Rose couldn't have been more excited. It was nearly two months since they had seen one another. Now it was the Easter holidays and they were getting together at Oralie's house.

Rose's mum dropped them off. Oralie's house was a neat semi-detached with a black front door and a birdbath in the garden. Rose's mum parked the car on the driveway and the girls jumped out. They rushed to knock at the front door and Oralie appeared from behind the curtains in the window, waving madly. Then she disappeared, presumably to come and let them in. A high yapping sound came from behind the door.

"That must be Sampson," said Yasmeen. Sampson was Oralie's new puppy.

"I can't wait to meet him," said Rose. She didn't have to wait long. Oralie opened the door and hugged the girls tight.

As soon as the door was closed, Oralie's dad opened the crate in the kitchen. A small beige, barking bundle shot out as if he'd been projected. He zoomed along the floor, little legs struggling on the shiny tiles. He ran in yapping circles around their legs and then sat on Oralie's feet. She scooped him into her arms and held him so that his four paws were pointing forwards.

"This is Sampson," she said, with a wide grin. "He goes in his crate every night or if he's getting overexcited. It's his safe space but he still loves to come out!"

Now that he was less of a blur, the girls could see that he was a compact little pug with a glossy fawn coat, a wrinkly black face and a curly tail.

Yasmeen stroked the top of Sampson's head and he gazed at her with large, round black eyes. "Awww, look at those eyes! He is so *cute!*"

"Don't let the eyes fool you – he is trouble," said Oralie's dad, standing with arms folded in the kitchen. Her mum was away in France, visiting relatives.

"He is a pest," confirmed Victor, who was Oralie's younger brother by just one year.

"Yes, but a cute, lovable pest," said Oralie, showering Sampson with kisses. He wriggled about in her hands and she put him back down on the floor where he sniffed at their feet.

"He loves children," said Oralie.

"I blame all this puppy business on you girls," said Mr Sands. "There was no going back after Wriggly came to stay!" Mr Sands had ended up looking after Rose's puppy, Wriggly, for one night while the girls were at summer camp.

"Sorry!" said Rose's mum. She knew Mr Sands was joking and that they all loved Sampson really.

Rose's mum said goodbye to Rose and the girls and Mr Sands led her through into the kitchen for a quick cup of tea before she drove home.

The girls followed Oralie upstairs to her room. Oralie had a big bedroom at the front of the house, which was full of stuff. There were posters plastered all over the walls, of pugs and llamas and dragons. Pompoms and birds and unicorn-shaped fairy lights hung from the ceiling. Her double bed was piled with cushions and cuddly toys. Towers of books wobbled in the corner.

"Wow, I love your room, Oralie. There is so much to look at," said Rose.

Oralie grinned. "Thanks. I tidied up for about three whole hours before you arrived."

The girls smiled and looked sideways at one another. The room was many things including fun and creative but it was certainly not tidy. Oralie caught the looks and laughed. "Yes, you should have seen it before!"

Amber picked up a framed photo of the four of them from the desk. She had given it to Oralie for Christmas. Yasmeen joined her. The desk was covered in notebooks and pen pots and a detective

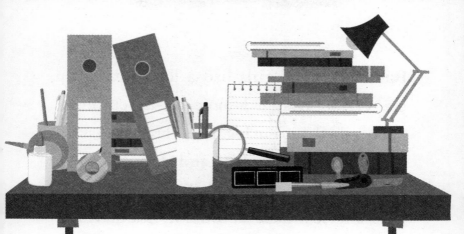

fingerprinting kit. There wasn't a clear spot anywhere. "Where do you do your homework, Oralie?"

"Oh, there's not enough room on the desk for boring things like homework! I do that on the floor!"

Still, there was enough room to squeeze in an extra three for a couple of nights. Amber would sleep top to tail with Oralie in her big double bed. The others would fit on blow-up beds on the floor.

But it was a while yet until bedtime.

Right now the girls had a lot to catch up on. Oralie arranged some of the cushions on her bed into a big pile. Then she gathered extra blankets and duvets. "It needs to be mega flumfy," she said.

Yasmeen looked confused. "Flumfy? Do you mean fluffy?"

"Or comfy?" asked Amber.

"Somewhere in between. Nice and flumfy," said Oralie, snuggling under a soft blanket.

Amber showed them all photos of her dog Fluffikins' puppies, who were born when they stayed with Amber during half term. They were now seven weeks old and unbelievably cute. The girls ahhed when they saw the pictures.

"They actually look like balls of fluff with tails now. Can you remember what they were like when they were newborns? They hardly had any fur at all," said Rose.

"We're keeping this one – the boy," said Amber as she pointed to the ginger puppy in the picture.

"What's his name?" asked Oralie.

Amber pulled a face. "My top tip is not to let a five-year-old choose the name. Leena choose *again* and she went for ... Puffy!"

The girls all laughed.

"I think the name Puffy is cute," said Yasmeen.

"Well she wanted to call him Prince Puffypaws, but my mum talked her out of that. Anyway, guess who's taking the other puppy – the girl?"

"Mrs Mack?" Oralie guessed correctly. Mrs Mack was Amber's next-door neighbour and, due to a little misunderstanding, Oralie had once wrongly accused her of dognapping! Luckily, they were all friends again now.

"Yep!" said Amber. "Mrs Mack chose the girl pup — the one that looks like a cotton wool ball with a tail. And can you guess what she is going to call her. . .?"

"Snowball!" chorused the girls. That was what Mrs Mack had insisted on calling Fluffikins, so they were certain that would be the name Mrs Mack chose for this dog too.

But Amber shook her head. "She called her Edna! After her sister. But she still calls Fluffikins Snowball."

The door opened a crack.

"Oh look, it's Sampson!" said Rose, as the little puppy trotted happily into the room. "He came all the way upstairs to find us! Those stairs must be like a mountain to him."

"He must have heard it was flumfy in here. Sampson *loves* flumfy stuff," said Oralie.

With a bit of help, Sampson scrabbled into bed with them. Oralie held him just like she did earlier, with his back towards her and his little paws sticking out.

She passed him, in the same position, to Yasmeen, who held him happily while they chatted. Then Yasmeen wanted to get a tissue from her bag so she passed Sampson to Amber.

"This is just like a game of pass the pug!" said Amber

"Well, I know what we're going to be doing this weekend then," said Rose. "It's going to be one long game of pass the pug!"

Oralie took a flying leap off the bed. "NO WAY! I can't believe I haven't told you yet! It's just with the new puppy and you arriving and everything I forgot to say. Every Easter we run a scavenger hunt and it's tomorrow! My dad works for the council so he has organized it all. It's going to be so much fun." Sometimes when Oralie was excited she forgot to take a breath.

"Sounds amazing," said Amber.

"Cool," said Yasmeen.

"What's a scavenger hunt?" asked Rose.

Chapter 2

Hiding Places

"A scavenger hunt is a competition. You do it in groups of families and friends. Everyone starts off at the church hall and follows clues around town," explained Oralie.

"That sounds fun, but why is it called a scavenger hunt?" asked Rose.

"You also *scavenge* stuff as you go.

You have a list of things that you need to find."

"Like what?"

"It could be absolutely anything. Little things, mainly. You can find them or buy them or go home and get them."

"I'm not sure I quite understand. . ."

"It will all make sense when we do it, I promise! Honestly, it will be the best day. You're going to love it."

"Can we all be on a team together?" asked Yasmeen

"Of course!" said Oralie.

"But haven't you seen all the lists and everything already?" asked Rose.

"No. Last year I helped dad make up the clues but this year I wanted us all to take part so we're not allowed to see anything. He's kept it all top secret."

"Maybe we could find the files and have a little peek," joked Amber.

Oralie shook her head. "No! That would spoil the fun. This year, I'm taking care of the prizes. Look." She felt around under the bed and pulled out a plastic crate filled with packets of mini eggs, chocolate chicks and a bigger, boxed Easter egg. She cradled the biggest one in her arms and stroked it lovingly. "A giant Easter egg. I want this one so much!"

Victor walked past Oralie's open door. "You'll just have to win it then. But remember you're going to have some competition from me and my friends!"

Oralie laughed at this. "Competition? I don't think so! You are competing against the four of us and we are all very shiny. When we get together, great things happen!"

Rose, Yasmeen and Amber ignored them and talked between themselves. It was best to stay out of sibling arguments.

Mr Sands appeared behind Victor.

Rose's mum had left to go home now.

"No squabbling, you two! Remember we have guests," he said.

"Us, squabble?" said Victor, innocently.

"Mmm. And make sure you look after those," said Mr Sands to Oralie, pointing to the prizes. "No midnight feasts tonight! No losing them, either. I know what you're like!"

"You can trust me, Dad. I've put them in my second-best hiding place."

"Why not your best-best hiding place?" asked Amber

"I didn't want it to be so good that I forgot where I put them. But maybe you're right. The first best hiding place would be better. Everyone leave the room! I'm going to move them."

The girls left the room and stood out

on the landing with Victor. Oralie kept the door firmly shut so there was no chance of anyone seeing where she put the prizes. There was the sound of furniture being dragged along and a loud "ouch!" from Oralie. After a short pause, she shouted "ready!" and the girls rushed back in. Victor shrugged and went back to his room to play with his action figures.

"The prizes are definitely safe now," said Oralie.

"Why have you got so many hiding places?" asked Yasmeen.

"Believe me, with a younger brother you need plenty of hiding places."

"It's the same with a little sister!" agreed Amber.

That evening, they took Sampson out for a walk and then Mr Sands cooked them a delicious meal.

Afterwards, Oralie sprang up straight away to stack the plates in the dishwasher. "We can't leave our plates out for a minute; otherwise Sampson jumps up to lick them clean. He is such a greedy boy."

That evening they settled down for a film and another game of pass the pug. They were all very excited about the scavenger hunt the next day – Oralie especially. "I can't wait until tomorrow. Honestly, you are going to love it so much."

Chapter 3

What Could Possibly Go Wrong?

In the morning, the girls knew that
Oralie would be the last one to get up.
They were all fully dressed by the time
she started to stir. Amber bent close to
her ear and said, "Oh no, we've missed
the scavenger hunt!"

"Wh-what?!" said Oralie, looking
frantically around her and leaping out of

bed. The girls all laughed and she checked the clock. "Hours to go! You are so mean!"

"We just didn't want you to miss it," said Yasmeen.

Oralie yawned and stretched. "We don't have to be there until later this morning but shall we get all our things ready?"

"What do we need?" asked Rose.

Oralie thought for a moment. "Good walking shoes. It might be quite a long trek around town."

"Trainers – tick," said Amber, ticking of the items with her fingers and thumb.

"A bag for collecting any treasures we find. . ."

"Backpacks – tick!"

"Water bottles in case we get thirsty. . ."

"Water bottles ready to fill – tick. What else?"

"I'm going to put some added extras in my backpack. Scissors, glue, sticky tape and my multi-tool gadget. Oh, and a dictionary." Oralie reached into the book tower and pulled out a book.

"Why, what do we need those for?"

"I don't know yet but I have done loads of these scavenger hunts before and you never know what you might need."

Oralie zipped up her backpack. "Right – all done. What could possibly go wrong?"

"Aren't you forgetting something?" said Yasmeen.

"Glue, sticky tape, spare pen, dictionary, multi-tool... No, I don't think so," said Oralie.

Amber folded her arms and looked mock stern. "Are you *sure*, Oralie?"

Oralie checked her bag again. "Yes, I think I'm sure! What do you mean?"

Rose giggled. "What about the prizes?"

Oralie hit her face with the heel of her hand. "The prizes – of course! We'd be in trouble without those!"

She pushed her door back and reached into the little cubbyhole behind. It used to be a fireplace and now was a rectangular gap with a curtain pulled across. Oralie's usual smile vanished from her face and she yanked the curtain all the way across.

"They've gone!"

The girls gathered immediately around her. "What do you mean?" asked Amber.

"The Easter eggs are missing! Someone has stolen the prizes!"

Chapter 4

Detective Work

Oralie sat cross-legged on the floor with her face buried in her hands. She was *devastated*. The girls gathered around her. They had never seen her like this before.

"I can't believe it's gone," she muttered, without lifting her head. "My dad is going to be so cross. He trusted me and I've let him down."

"Are you sure you are looking in the right hiding place?" asked Yasmeen.

Oralie rubbed her face with her hands and looked up. "I checked all my hiding places. Hiding place number four is up in the cupboard behind my roller boots. Hiding place number three is in this hollowed-out book. That was too small. Hiding place number two is under the bed. But hiding place one is just here in this cubbyhole behind the door. I know it looks obvious but no one ever spots it when the door is open. And I *know* I put the prizes in hiding place number one."

As Oralie was talking them through the hiding places, the girls checked to make sure she hadn't missed something. The Easter eggs did seem to have gone.

"This is really odd," said Yasmeen. "Chocolate can't vanish."

Oralie sighed. "Well, it has. There's no reason to even go to the scavenger hunt now. What's the point?"

Amber lifted up Oralie's chin. "Come on, Oralie, I thought you were training to be a detective?"

"I *was* until the unfortunate Mrs Mack episode. I have sort of given it up since then." Oralie had accused Mrs Mack of stealing Amber's dog, who had luckily turned up in the end.

"Well, maybe now is the time to give up giving up! We need your detective skills," said Yasmeen.

"Who do you think is the most likely person to have taken the prizes?" asked Rose.

At the prospect of a new case, detective Oralie looked suddenly alert again. "Burglars!" she cried.

Yasmeen raised an eyebrow. "Do we really think it was a burglar? Let's think about this logically. The only time we left this room was when we were watching the film last night. Would burglars have broken into the house without us noticing, come up to your room, ignored all your other valuables and stolen the prizes?"

Oralie thought about this for a moment. "It does seem unlikely."

"And if you definitely haven't misplaced the prizes—"

"I definitely haven't misplaced the

prizes…"

"Then we have to think logically about who might have taken them."

Oralie thought about this for another moment. "Victor! I'm going to his room right now to get them back!" She sprang up and rushed for the bedroom door.

Yasmeen stood in her way. "Think about it *logically*, I said! We can't just rush off and accuse someone."

Oralie sighed. "OK, thinking *logically*, if it wasn't burglars then it must be someone else in the house. Was it you, Rose?"

Rose shook her head. "Of course not!"

"Amber? Yasmeen?"

"No!" they both protested.

"And I think I can safely say that it isn't my dad as he *bought* the prizes.

There is only one person left in the house and that person is my brother, which is why I'm going round there right now..."

Rose put a hand on Oralie's arm. "Only one other *person* left but there is another possibility. Someone who we know is mischievous, cheeky and loves sweet things. Oralie, I think I know who the prize thief might be."

Chapter 5

The Burglar

In the end, all the evidence pointed in one direction. They found traces of muddy paw prints and ripped-up pieces of cardboard box scattered down the stairs. They followed the trail through the hallway and the kitchen and out into the garden.

Over by the shed, was Sampson,

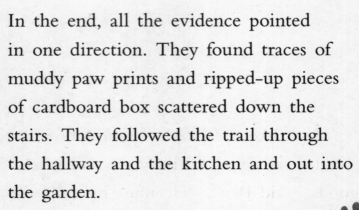

frantically digging in the loose earth
of the flowerbed with his front paws.
Scattered around him were packs of mini
eggs and chicks. He looked up guiltily as
they approached.

"Look – we've caught him red-
handed!" said Yasmeen.

"More like red-pawed," said Amber.
"He was trying to bury the stolen
goods," said Rose. "He must have taken
them last night when we were watching

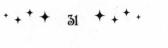

the film."

"Sampson – how could you?" shouted
Oralie, rushing towards him.

Sampson stuck out his little pink
tongue and panted. Digging was
obviously hard work. His face and front
legs were covered in earth and he looked
cuter than ever. Oralie sighed. "It's
impossible to be cross with you."

Amber investigated the buried treasure.
"There are only a few packets of mini
eggs here. Where are the rest?"

They found the big egg and the rest
of the packets in Sampson's crate, hidden
behind his cushion.

"Oh, Sampson! What have you done?"
said Amber.

Oralie scooped up all the prizes. "I'm
glad I didn't blame Victor. Thanks for
stopping me. I sometimes get a bit carried

away."

"That's OK. You just wanted to find the prizes. It's only natural," said Yasmeen.

"I can't bring myself to tell my dad. He told me so many times to look after the prizes — what am I going to do?"

Rose put her arm around Oralie. "Your dad will understand. It wasn't your fault. It was an accident."

"But he trusted me to look after the prizes and I *failed*. I should have used my fourth-best hiding place and then Sampson wouldn't have been able to find them."

"Maybe your fourth-best hiding place should become your first-best hiding place," suggested Rose with a wink.

"Definitely. I'm never hiding anything behind the door ever again."

"Maybe it will help if we go to your

dad with a plan. If we let him know how we are going to put things right, then he can't get angry, can he?"

Rose couldn't imagine Mr Sands getting angry – he was such a calm and friendly man.

"He won't be angry – he'll be disappointed, which is worse, isn't it? A plan sounds like a good way forward but I have no idea how we are going to fix this one. Any ideas, anyone?"

"Let me have a little think," said Rose.

Chapter 6

Fixing It

Oralie's dad wasn't cross after all. He could see how upset Oralie was and it wasn't really her fault. "It's this puppy — I've said all along that he is a pest."

"Can we go up to the supermarket and get another one?"

"Another puppy? I think one is quite enough!" joked Mr Sands.

Oralie put her hands on her hips. "You know what I mean. Not another puppy — another prize."

"No! We have a budget from the school. We can't just go out and buy more prizes. The winners this year will just have to be happy with their certificates."

"We can't just give certificates. Everyone knows that there is an Easter egg prize. It's tradition! And if there isn't and it's all my fault it will be *terrible*."

"They'll understand," said Mr Sands.

"They *won't!*" cried Oralie.

The girls all looked at each other. They didn't like seeing Oralie this upset. Rose turned the rescued Easter egg around in her hands, inspecting it. "Maybe there's a way round it. The egg is still in its foil and in the plastic container."

"Yes, Sampson only damaged the cardboard, not the egg itself," said Yasmeen.

"Which is a good job," said Mr Sands. "Sampson would have made himself very sick indeed if he had eaten any of the chocolate."

"But we can't give the egg away just in the clear plastic. It doesn't look like much of a prize, does it?"

Rose shook her head slowly. "That's not what I'm thinking. We still have loads of mini eggs and chocolate chicks. Do you have any breakfast cereal?

"Yes, we do. "

"I can guess what you're thinking of," said Amber.

Oralie looked confused. "I'm glad somebody can, because I haven't got a clue!"

"Chocolate nests!" said Rose. "We could use the chocolate to make them and decorate them with the eggs. They would look pretty and they are Eastery as well."

Yasmeen clapped her hands together. "I'm not sure that Eastery is a word, but I think they'd make the perfect presents."

Oralie brightened up for the first time since the prizes had gone missing. "Easter nests ... good idea! What do you think, Dad?"

Mr Sands smiles. "I think it's a great idea. You girls will have to do some of the cooking

on your own, though; I have other things to prepare. And you'll have to do it quickly, too – we have to leave for the scavenger hunt in one hour."

Chapter 7

New Prizes

Mr Sands started them off by heating up some water in a saucepan. He showed them how to break up the chocolate and melt it in a bowl over the pan of hot water.

"How many prizes do we need?" Oralie asked her dad.

"Well, there is obviously the main

prize for the overall winner and then we're going to give three other prizes, too."

"What are they for?"

"That would be telling," said Mr Sands, with a wink. "They are surprise prizes."

"Sur*prizes,*" said Yasmeen.

"So four all together," said Oralie.

Mr Sands nodded. "That's right. Now that we've done the stove stuff," he said, switching it off, "I'm going to leave you to it. I need to make sure that I have all my clues together. Try not to make too much of a mess!"

Then, to make things quicker, they each did one job. "Like in a factory," said Rose.

Oralie crushed Weetabix with a rolling pin and mixed it into the chocolate.

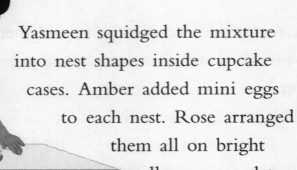

Yasmeen squidged the mixture into nest shapes inside cupcake cases. Amber added mini eggs to each nest. Rose arranged them all on bright yellow paper plates, with chocolate chicks and bows. Rose was right, they were very Eastery, even if it wasn't a word.

"Phew — I think we've finished!" said Rose, wiping her hands on a tea towel.

Victor popped his head into the kitchen and grinned. "Can I lick the spoon?" he asked.

Rose began handing it to him but Oralie stepped in and whipped it away.

"No you cannot lick the spoon! Spoon licking

is only for chefs and you haven't done any of the work." She popped the spoon into her mouth. "Mmm, delicious!"

"There is enough in the bowl for the other three chefs," she said, pointing towards the bowl on the table. But a certain little pug had already discovered it. He had somehow got on top of the kitchen table, tipped the bowl on its side and was putting chocolatey pawprints all over the worktop .

"Sampson!" said Oralie, whipping the bowl away from him before he could eat any. "Sorry, it's too late! I don't think any of you will want this now his paws have been in it."

Victor walked out of the kitchen with his hands in his pockets then turned around. "Never mind, I'll have loads of chocolate nests when my team wins later!"

Oralie rolled her eyes. "Brothers!"

Sampson was leaving little chocolately paw prints on the table and the bench. Rose chased after him with a cloth, wiping down the kitchen surfaces. "All finished but the nests will take a little while to set."

"Perfect – we'll leave them here for a few minutes which will give us time to get ready."

Amber eyed Sampson suspiciously. "This time, let's keep them out of reach of a certain little pug!"

They called Oralie's dad, who put

the chocolate nests up in a high kitchen cupboard. There was no way Sampson could reach them up there. "Whatever you do, don't forget to take them to the scavenger hunt," he said.

Chapter 8

The Hunt

The girls didn't forget the prizes. The
Sands lived close to town, so they walked
in, each carrying a plate. Victor held
Sampson's lead.

Rose smiled at Sampson trotting along
and sniffing everything along the way.
He didn't seem in much of a hurry. "I
didn't know that Sampson was coming

on the scavenger hunt."

"He comes everywhere. He doesn't like being left on his own," said Oralie.

"Awww, like a baby," said Yasmeen.

"Are we nearly at the church hall now?" asked Amber.

Oralie nodded. "It's just around the corner."

"I can smell the chocolate nests!" said Yasmeen. "They are making my mouth water."

"We could always forget the scavenger hunt, go to the park and eat these instead!" joked Oralie.

"I heard that!" said Mr Sands.

The girls and the prizes made it to the church hall intact. There was a fridge inside, where they could keep the prizes cool.

All the groups registered at a table in

the hall. The girls queued until it was their turn.

"Group name?"

"The Treasure Box," said the girls, without hesitation. That had been their group name at camp and it worked just as well now.

They were given a plastic coated number four, a map of the town, a *To Find* list and a sheet of clues.

Victor and his friends came past waving a number three. "We'll be leaving before you!" he said.

"It doesn't matter what time you leave," said Oralie. "You are judged on the time you take to complete the hunt. You should watch your back – we might catch you up."

"No you won't," said Victor, "We've got these." He pointed to a pile of scooters stacked by the door.

"That's why we're called the Scooting Scavengers," said his friend Harry.

Oralie gasped. "That's cheating! Dad, Victor's friends have brought scooters. Isn't that cheating?"

"No, it's absolutely fine – stop squabbling with your brother!" said Mr Sands.

Amber patted Oralie on the arm. "I don't honestly think it will make too much difference. They have to stop and answer clues anyway, don't they?"

"I suppose so," grumbled Oralie, but she still threw dark looks in Victor's direction.

Once all the teams were registered, the hunt began. Each group left five minutes apart so that they couldn't copy each other.

The Treasure Box would be the fourth group to leave the hall. They used the waiting time to get organized.

Oralie waved the sheets of paper they were given at the desk. "Who's going to hold the clues?"

"Can I? I've brought a clipboard," said Yasmeen,

delving into her backpack.

"You brought a clipboard all the way from home?" asked Oralie in disbelief.

"Yes. I like clipboards."

The other girls laughed.

"Can I take the *To Find* list?" said Amber.

"And I'll take the bag to put them in," said Oralie.

"In that case, I'm going to be the only one with a free hand. Can I walk Sampson?" asked Rose

"Of course!"

"What sort of items are on the find list?" asked Rose.

Amber ran her finger down the sheet. "The first thing on the list is: a daisy."

"You have to be creative," explained Oralie. "So that could be a daisy hairclip or a daisy T-shirt or a nametag belonging to someone called Daisy..."

"Or ... a daisy!" said Rose, pointing to the daisies in the churchyard

"Group number four – The Treasure Box!" called Oralie's dad. It was their turn to start the scavenger hunt.

Rose rushed straight outside to pick a daisy from the churchyard and the others followed close behind. Oralie laughed and opened the clear plastic bag so that Rose could drop in the daisy. "Some of them will be a bit trickier than that, I'm sure!"

They made their way to the church gates. Group three was already out of sight.

"So, what's the first clue, Yasmeen?" asked Oralie.

Yasmeen cleared her throat and read in a singsong voice, "Leave the church hall and head west."

"West? Is that left or right?" asked Amber.

"Well it depends on which way you're facing, doesn't it?"

"Does it?"

Oralie fiddled with her multi-tool gadget. "I though there was a compass here somewhere, but I can't find it."

Yasmeen looked up. "Isn't that a weathervane on top of the church hall? Look, the W is pointing that way, so west must be a right turn here."

"I hope it's going to get easier that this, or I'm going to give up now," said Rose.

"Give up! I don't think so," said Oralie. "Not with Victor's team up ahead."

As they walked along the street,

Amber read the next clue.

"One for sorrow, so they say, but breakfast here will make your day."

"Oh no, it's in riddles! You didn't tell me it would be in riddles. It makes no sense!" said Rose.

Yasmeen peeked over Amber's shoulder. "It does! Think about it logically. *One for sorrow, two for joy* ... that's the famous rhyme about magpies, isn't it?"

"How do you know so many rhymes, Yasmeen? I can never remember any," said Amber.

Yasmeen had remembered the whole of the "make new friends" rhyme back at summer camp. Now she was reciting the rest of this magpie rhyme. *"Three for a girl, four for a boy. . .* It's definitely magpies. Is there anything to do with magpies around here? The name of a house or a shop—"

"Yes!' shrieked Oralie and pulled Amber by the arm. "Quick – down here!" She shot off down a side street. The girls all followed, with Sampson dragging the lead and barking all the way. Oralie stood in front of a small but busy café. On the sign above the window was a black bird and letters spelling out *The Magpie Café*. *"Breakfast here will make your day!* It makes complete sense after all!"

Amber wrote it down then pointed with her pencil to the next line on the paper. "There's a question here." She read aloud:

"It may be 'one for sorrow', but what's 'five for'?"

"Come on Yasmeen, what comes next in the rhyme?"

Yasmeen laughed. "I should definitely

know this one! It's silver. *Five for silver, six for gold and seven for a secret ready to be told.*"

Amber wrote down silver (which happened to be Yasmeen's surname) on the sheet and read out the next clue.

"Take fourteen steps down the street and turn to your left. What is the name of the road?"

They wrote down *North Street*.

"Now take the second turning on your right and walk to the end of the road. Draw the view ahead."

At the end of the road stood an archway and a statue of a man with an old-fashioned hat, pointing into the air.

"This one's for you," said Yasmeen, handing the clipboard to Rose, who was the best artist.

While Rose was drawing, Oralie

looked at Amber's *To Find* list. "We mustn't forget to get these things. It is a scavenger hunt after all. So far we only have one daisy. What's left on the list?"

Chapter 9

Scavenging

Amber read out the list.

TO FIND
(Be as creative as you like!)
A bone
A four-leaved clover
Something beginning with 'Q'
Something old

Something shiny
A tomato
A doughnut

"Hmmm, they don't sound that easy," said Oralie.

Yasmeen looked around. "We could go to the museum and see if they have any bones. They might have something old, as well."

"But wouldn't those things be on display for us to look at − not to buy?" said Amber.

"You're probably right. I know − Sampson can help us," said Oralie, wiggling the little tag off his collar. It had his name and number on it and was in the shape of a bone.

"Hooray, a bone!" said Yasmeen. "Now we need to make especially sure we don't lose him."

"I may have lost the prizes, but I'm definitely not going to lose my puppy!" said Oralie, giving Sampson a stroke. Then she rustled in her purse and took out a photo of her dad. "You can tick *Something old* off the list as well. My dad - he's very old!"

"But isn't he judging this?" said Yasmeen.

"He'll think it's funny. I hope," said Oralie.

Rose finished a detailed drawing of the sculpture and they ticked it off the list. Then they followed the next clues along the high street and into the town park. They had to keep Sampson well away from the ducks.

Yasmeen looked down at her feet as they walked. "There's a load of clover here."

"But we need a four-leaved clover and there's no time to look. We could search for hours and never find one," said Amber

Rose nodded. "Can you pass the sticky tape, Oralie?"

She plucked two ordinary three-leaved clovers from the grass and pulled a leaf from one. She stuck it with the other clover on a piece of paper to make it appear four-leaved.

Yasmeen wasn't sure. "Isn't that cheating?" she asked.

"Of course not – we are encouraged to be creative!" said Oralie, pointing at the sheet.

Amber twiddled the "four leaved" clover paper between her fingers and dropped it in the treasure bag. "I've got a joke: what's the difference between a four-leaved clover, a three-leaved clover and a roll of sticky tape?"

"I don't know," chorused the other girls.

"What *is* the difference between a four-leaved clover, a three-leaved clover and a roll of sticky tape?" asked Rose.

"A four-leaved clover has four leaves and a three-leaved clover has three leaves."

"O...K...! and what about the roll of sticky tape?" asked Yasmeen.

Rose smiled. "Ah, that's where you get stuck!"

They all laughed and carried on with the trail.

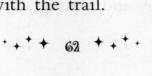

Oralie continued adding items to the bag as they went. For *A tomato*, Oralie took a crumpled tomato ketchup crisp packet out of her pocket and cut out the picture on the front. "Perfect!"

And for *Something beginning with* Q she flicked through the dictionary, found the Q section and put in the rest of the crisp packet as a bookmark.

"Lots of things beginning with Q! And it saves us going to the supermarket and looking for quail's eggs," she said.

For *Something shiny*. Oralie put in her bracelet.

Rose gasped. "But that's precious!"

"Don't worry – we get everything back afterwards."

"Now all that's left is the doughnut," said Amber. Luckily, the clues seemed to be leading them back into town.

"We can buy a doughnut at the bakery," said Oralie.

But when they reached the bakery, they had completely sold out.

"You're the fourth group of children that's come in here looking for doughnuts," said the man behind the counter. "A group of boys bought three whole boxes! Is it National Doughnut day or something?"

Oralie gasped. "I can't believe it! Victor's group are trying to sabotage us by buying all the doughnuts. That's so unfair!"

"Don't worry," said Yasmeen. "I'm sure we'll think of something."

Oralie looked around. "It would be a shame to walk in here and not buy anything. Shall we get a cake while we're here?"

They bought four chocolate brownies, which they quickly ate leaving the shop.

Rose took a huge bite of hers, made a sound that was something like "Dounnunn" and started taking down her hair, which was swept back in a bun.

"What's she talking about?" asked Yasmeen.

Rose swallowed her mouthful and said "hair doughnut!" She whipped something out of her hair and held in the air, triumphantly. It was the spongey device that she used to put her hair up.

"Well done — I knew we'd find a creative solution," said Oralie.

"And we got cake as well!" Amber laughed and finished her brownie

They had just a few more clues to complete.

"We need to be quick! Come on Sampson – you're slowing us down," said Oralie.

"Awww, he's doing his best. He's only got little legs," said Amber.

They turned left to follow a clue to the library but spotted Victor's group scooting past in the other direction.

"I think they're lost," said Oralie, with a laugh.

"Either that, or we are!" said Rose.

Chapter 10

Sur-prizes

The girls made it back to the hall and dropped off their plastic bags and clue sheets. Then they found the refreshments table and filled their plates with triangular sandwiches, carrot sticks and crisps. Sampson had water and some of his special treats.

"All this walking has given me an appetite," said Oralie.

"You always have an appetite," said Yasmeen, with a smile.

It took nearly another hour for all the groups to make it back to the hall. Once they were all there and the judges had checked all the answers, Mr Sands brought out the Easter nests and clapped his hands for silence. "Soon, we will be giving out the winners' certificate, but before that, we have a few runners' up prizes to present."

He talked a bit more about how they'd all done really well and thanked all the people that had helped organize the hunt. The girls were really keen to know if they had won a prize. "I can just taste the chocolate now," whispered Oralie.

"The prize for the quickest time goes to ... the Scooting Scavengers!"

Victor and his friends cheered,

punched the air and went to collect their chocolate nests.

Oralie narrowed her eyes. "They wouldn't have been so quick if they hadn't been on their scooters," she said.

Amber rubbed Oralie's back. "It's OK, just breathe slowly," she joked.

"The prize for the best team name goes to ... Big Steve and the Superhero Scavengers!"

Everyone laughed as Big Steve and his team mates went to collect their prize. They had all dressed in masks and capes like superheroes.

"The prize for the most original interpretation of the list goes to ... the Treasure Box!"

"NO WAY!" shouted Oralie. The girls leapt up and rushed up to get their chocolate nests.

"Yasmeen, are you crying again?"

Yasmeen wiped her eyes. "I was just surprised. I didn't think we'd win anything."

"Nor did I. I don't even know what our prize means," said Oralie. "Not that I'm bothered," she said, through a mouthful of chocolate nest.

"Most original interpretation means that we didn't choose the most obvious things," said Yasmeen.

Rose laughed. "Apart from the daisy, of course," she said.

The overall winners were a family with two small boys. Amber heard one of the boys say, "These are the best prizes ever," as he walked back from the prize table.

"Makes it all worth it, doesn't it?" said Oralie.

Victor and his friends also enjoyed

their chocolate nests.

"These are yum. They were worth waiting for," said Victor.

"I can't believe you are eating chocolate nests after eating all those doughnuts earlier," said Oralie.

Victor looked puzzled. "All *which* doughnuts?"

"The doughnuts you bought from the shop earlier to stop us getting hold of them!"

"That wasn't us. They were already gone by the time we got to the bakery. It must have been Big Steve and his group."

"Really?"

"Really. We didn't even get half of the stuff on the list. Or do the clues. We just whizzed around as quickly as we could."

"OK, sorry," said Oralie.

Yasmeen gaped in surprise. "Did I just hear that Victor's group were innocent after all?"

Oralie laughed. "I know, I know. Find out the facts *before* accusing people of crimes. I am trying. But it's different with brothers, isn't it?"

Chapter 11

Best Friends For Ever

The sun was out, so Oralie, Amber, Rose and Yasmeen took their chocolate nests out into the churchyard. They found the daisy-sprinkled patch of grass where Rose had picked her flower.

Oralie finished hers and licked her fingers. "For once, Victor's right. Those chocolate nests are yum."

"I agree. They are better than boring eggs would have been," said Amber.

"Even if we do say so ourselves," said Rose, giggling.

Oralie opened the plastic bag and began returning everything to its rightful location. "We don't need this any more," she said, throwing the daisy on to the grass.

"Yes we do," said Yasmeen, picking up the abandoned daisy. "This is perfect for making a lamb's tail."

She lopped the tops off a few more daisies and threaded them on to the first stalk. It looked like a white, fluffy lamb's tail.

"Here's your hair doughnut, Rose. I bet that won us some originality points."

She put the tag back on Sampson's collar and then took out her shiny gold bracelet. She inspected it, turning it around in a full circle. "A couple of tiny scratches. I'm not sure it's completely circular any more but it's survived a lot."

"Llama trekking!" said Rose.

"Indoor ice skating!" said Yasmeen.

"Crime solving!" said Amber.

Oralie laughed and lay flat on her back on the grass. "Yes, and now sweet-trailing, nest-building and scavenger-hunting as well. How are everyone else's bracelets looking after all those adventures?"

The other girls lay down on the grass with Oralie, heads together and legs stretching out like a star. They reached out their arms to compare bracelets, which shone in the sunshine. Rose gold, yellow gold, silver, and orange.

"Make new friends and keep the old,
Amber, Silver, Rose and Gold." sang
Yasmeen.

They all smiled at one another,
turning their heads from side to side on
the grass.

Rose sat up and turned to face the
other girls. "Do you realize we've seen
each other in Summer, Winter and
now Spring?"

The others
all sat up with her.

"Four friends, four seasons, four shiny metals," said Amber.

"Nearly a whole year of friendship!" added Oralie. "Shall we do the same next year?"

"Yes, and the year after that!" cried Yasmeen.

"And the year after that!" joined in Rose.

Sampson ran in a circle around them, barking at the excitement.

"He agrees! Next time we meet, all the dogs should come too," suggested Amber.

"A big doggy picnic!" said Yasmeen.

"Yes!" said Rose. "Wriggly and Sampson would be best friends, running around and barking. Mabel and Fluffikins would snuggle up together. What do you think?"

Oralie gave Sampson a stroke. "I think they would all be best friends together, like us."

The girls grinned, held hands and lay flat on the grass again.

"BEST FRIENDS FOR EVER!"

Keep an eye out for Rose Gold and
Friends: Amber's Mystery Sleepover:

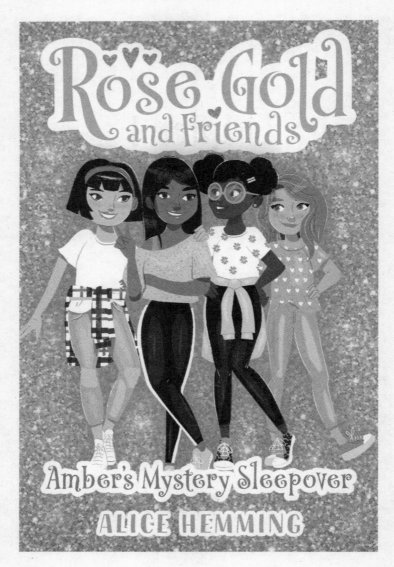

Chapter 1

Back Together

"Thank you for having us, Mrs Beau," said Rose shyly to Amber's mum.

"Do call me Monisha. And it's lovely to have you here. What with four girls, two boys, a dog, and a coop full of chickens, there's always room for a few more!"

Rose, Yasmeen and Oralie had just

arrived at Amber's house, where they were staying for a few nights. Amber and her mum, who looked like an older version of Amber with shorter hair, were giving them a tour.

"Your house is lovely!" said Rose, gazing around appreciatively

"It is as big as BigToes Hall! And as beautiful!" agreed Oralie.

The friends had met at Camp Bickrose (which they called Camp BigToes) during the summer. They got on so well that they met up again at Yasmeen's house for the Christmas holidays and now at Amber's during February half term.

"It might be big and beautiful but there is *nothing* to do here!" said Amber. "That's one reason I came to summer camp. And to get away from my brothers and sisters! Speaking of which, my little sister Leena is excited about meeting you all." Amber pointed to a little girl hiding behind Monisha. Leena looked like a younger version of Amber with longer hair. "This is my dolly," she said, holding out a tatty fabric doll.

"Your doll is very pretty," said Yasmeen, kindly.

"Would you like to play?" asked Leena.

Monisha stepped in. "Yasmeen will play later. Leena, would you like to help me decorate some yummy biscuits?"

Leena nodded

and smiled as Monisha whisked her away. Amber mouthed, "Thank you."

"She would want to play all day otherwise," Amber explained to the others. "My other brothers and sisters are bigger. Two are away at university. Sara and Omesh are upstairs. They are teenagers."

She beckoned the girls through the hallway. "Come on, let me show you the Snug, where we're going to sleep!"

The Snug was a huge family room at the back of the house with glass doors facing the garden. There was a big TV, computer, games, sofa and some colourful beanbags. Four camp beds were already set up on the floor but there was still space around them. The girls had all brought sleeping bags and pillows. Rose started to unroll hers on the bed in the left-hand corner. "Let's sleep on the same sides as we did at camp and at Yasmeen's," suggested Rose.

"Good plan," said Yasmeen, putting her sleeping bag on one of the beds on the right side of the room.

There was a sign balanced on an art easel near the glass doors. At the top, it read *Welcome to Camp BigBeau* (Beau was Amber's surname). Oralie ran over to take a look. "Oh look, you've even made a timetable like we had at camp!" she said.

"Monday: midnight feast, film.
Tuesday: chocolate, film.
Wednesday: pizza, film.
Thurday: pizza, film.
Friday: home :(:("

Amber laughed. "It's only a joke,

though. We can do whatever we like!"

On the sofa was what looked like a fluffy white cushion with eyes. It turned out to be a dog, white but with golden patches on her back and golden ears, and a pink tongue. She yapped excitedly. Rose sat down and began stroking soothingly and Amber joined her on the other side. "This is Fluffikins."

"What is she?" asked Yasmeen.

"She is a big fluffball. She is lovely
but lately, she's been getting a bit lazy.
Mum says we're going to put her on a
diet."

"I meant what breed?" asked
Yasmeen, joining them on the sofa.

"She is a Pomeranian. A Pom. Leena
says she looks like a pompom too! Leena
is the one who called her Fluffikins,
because she is the fluffiest thing we ever
seen."

"Close your eyes!" said Oralie,
suddenly. The girls all closed their eyes.
They could hear Oralie rummaging
about in her bag.

"Can we open them yet?" asked
Amber after a few moments.

"Ten more seconds," said Oralie.
There was the sound of a zip. "Open
your eyes now!"

Look out for the other Rose Gold books...

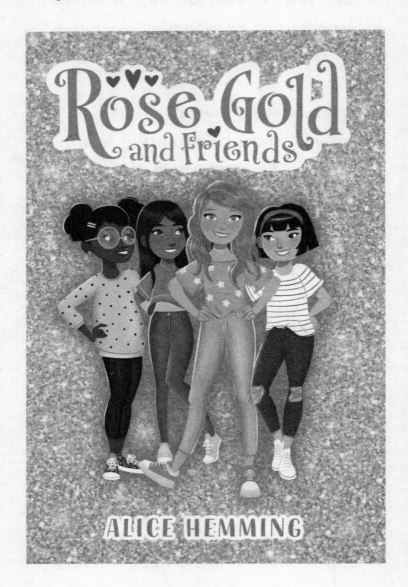

Rose Gold
and Friends

ALICE HEMMING

Rose Gold
and Friends

Yasmeen's Winter Fun

ALICE HEMMING

Rose Gold
and Friends

Amber's Mystery Sleepover

ALICE HEMMING